A Tale of Two Sisters

★ Also by ★

Debbie Dadey

MERMAID TALES

BOOK 1: *TROUBLE AT TRIDENT ACADEMY*

BOOK 2: *BATTLE OF THE BEST FRIENDS*

BOOK 3: *A WHALE OF A TALE*

BOOK 4: *DANGER IN THE DEEP BLUE SEA*

BOOK 5: *THE LOST PRINCESS*

BOOK 6: *THE SECRET SEA HORSE*

BOOK 7: *DREAM OF THE BLUE TURTLE*

BOOK 8: *TREASURE IN TRIDENT CITY*

BOOK 9: *A ROYAL TEA*

Coming Soon

BOOK 11: *THE POLAR BEAR EXPRESS*

Mermaid Tales

★Debbie Dadey★

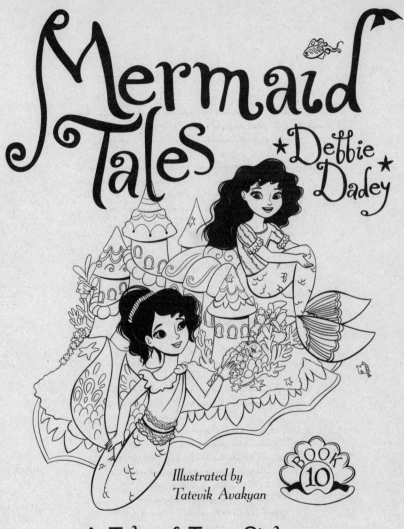

Illustrated by
Tatevik Avakyan

BOOK 10

A Tale of Two Sisters

ALADDIN
NEW YORK   LONDON   TORONTO   SYDNEY   NEW DELHI

This book is a work of fiction. Any references to historical events, real people, or real places are used fictitiously. Other names, characters, places, and events are products of the author's imagination, and any resemblance to actual events or places or persons, living or dead, is entirely coincidental.

ALADDIN

An imprint of Simon & Schuster Children's Publishing Division

1230 Avenue of the Americas, New York, NY 10020

This Aladdin paperback edition January 2015

Text copyright © 2015 by Debbie Dadey

Illustrations copyright © 2015 by Tatevik Avakyan

All rights reserved, including the right of reproduction in whole or in part in any form.

ALADDIN is a trademark of Simon & Schuster, Inc.,

and related logo is a registered trademark of Simon & Schuster, Inc.

Also available in an Aladdin hardcover edition.

For information about special discounts for bulk purchases,

please contact Simon & Schuster Special Sales at 1-866-506-1949

or business@simonandschuster.com.

The Simon & Schuster Speakers Bureau can bring authors to your live event.

For more information or to book an event contact the

Simon & Schuster Speakers Bureau at 1-866-248-3049

or visit our website at www.simonspeakers.com.

Book design by Karin Paprocki

The text of this book was set in Belucian Book.

Manufactured in the United States of America 0415 OFF

4 6 8 10 9 7 5 3

Library of Congress Control Number 2014936935

ISBN 978-1-4814-0258-3 (hc)

ISBN 978-1-4814-0257-6 (pbk)

ISBN 978-1-4814-0259-0 (eBook)

To my brothers, Frank Gibson
and David Gibson

In memory of Christin Mary Barilla,
who loved children

★ ★ ★ ★

Acknowledgment

Thanks to the lovely people at the Doylestown Bookshop for all your support!

Cast of Characters

Shelly

Echo

Kiki

Pearl

Rocky

Contents

Too Many Tail Flips!

CHO REEF TUCKED IN HER fins and flipped two times in a row.

"That was tails down the best flip I've ever seen!" Shelly Siren told her. The girls floated outside Echo's shell in the early morning before school.

Echo grinned as she stretched her pink tail. "Thanks! I've been practicing a lot lately. The Tail Flippers are performing a new routine for Parent Night, and Coach Barnacle wants it to be perfect. If anyone misses even one practice, they won't be able to perform!"

The Tail Flippers were Trident Academy's gymnastics and dance group. Echo was thrilled that she had made the team this year, and she couldn't wait to show off her new moves on Parent Night.

Echo and Shelly were in the third grade at Trident Academy, a prestigious school for third through tenth graders. They both lived close to the school, but merstudents from faraway waters lived in the dorms. Many families would be crossing the ocean to visit for Parent Night. Besides the Tail Flippers, the Pep Band and the Trident Chorus would perform, and there would even be a student art show.

"Coach Barnacle wants the Shell Wars team to play a scrimmage that night too,"

Shelly said. "It will be strange playing in front of so many merpeople." Shell Wars was a game where players took turns whacking shells with whalebones. Echo knew that Shelly was proud to be part of the team.

Echo grinned. "I've never flipped in front of so many merpeople before! It sounds so exciting." Like Shelly, Echo was used to performing in front of her fellow mer-students, but not strangers.

"I just know you'll be totally wavy!" Shelly said.

"Maybe I'd better practice even more," Echo said. "There are only a few days left before Parent Night."

Echo's sister, Crystal, stuck her head out of a window of their family's shell.

"Echo, you'd better hurry. It's almost time for school."

Crystal had the same dark hair and eyes as Echo, but she was two years older. Crystal stared at Echo's sparkly T-shirt. "Hey! Isn't that *my* shirt you're wearing?"

Echo groaned. Lately Crystal was always telling her what to do.

"No, it *used* to be yours," Echo told her. "Mom gave it to me because it doesn't fit you anymore. And I'm just going to do one more flip."

"Fine," Crystal replied, "but don't blame me if you're late." She paused. "Oh, hi, Shelly. I like your necklace."

Shelly waved. "Thanks. Yours is pretty too."

With that, Crystal swam off in a burst of bubbles.

"You are so lucky to have an older sister." Shelly sighed. "Crystal is the coolest. She's always so nice to me." Shelly's parents had died when she was a small fry, so she lived alone with her grandfather.

Echo shook her head. "I wish I was an only child like you, for sharks' sake. You never have anyone bossing you around. Plus, you don't have to wear someone else's old hand-me-downs! I hardly ever get anything new of my very own."

Shelly shrugged, and Echo shook out her tail. She was tired of talking about Crystal! Instead she took a huge leap and flipped in a loop three times. Echo was going so fast that she tailspinned into a rather large rock.

"Argh!" she shrieked, landing with a thud.

"Are you all right?" Shelly cried, rushing up beside her merfriend.

"I think so," Echo replied. She checked her tail and didn't find any loose scales.

"Thank Neptune you aren't hurt!" Shelly said. "But Crystal was right. We're going to be late to school. Shake your fins and let's get swimming."

Echo nodded and pushed back her hair, only to discover that her glittering plankton bow was missing.

"Just a merminute," she said. "Can you help me find my bow? It must have fallen off." Echo rarely went to school without something sparkly decorating her dark curly hair.

Echo and Shelly searched the ocean floor for the bioluminescent plankton.

"I found it!" Shelly said, holding up the glowing creature.

But Echo had found something too.

"Sweet seaweed!" she screeched as she lifted a rock the size of a small jellyfish. "Check this out!"

2

Stages

THE TWO MERGIRLS STARED at the strange object in front of them.

"What is it?" Shelly asked.

Echo shrugged. "I don't know, but it's the waviest thing I've ever seen."

"Do you think it's from humans?" Shelly asked.

Echo smiled. "I hope so!" She loved everything about people and collected objects that might have once belonged to humans, but she had never found anything like this before.

This object, whatever it was, had two chains that were connected by a round disk. It looked like it was made of pure gold. It sparkled and shone.

"Uh-oh. It's getting late!" Shelly warned. "We'd better get to school before Mrs. Karp makes us shark bait!"

Echo knew her friend was right, but she hated to leave her new find. It was so pretty that she just wanted to keep staring at it all day.

"Let me put this in my room. I'll be really quick," she promised.

As fast as a sailfish, Echo swam into her shell and looked around for a place to put her new treasure. She decided to hide it behind a sponge chair in her bedroom. Now that Echo had something that was all hers, she didn't want Crystal taking it.

The mergirls got to their third-grade classroom just as the conch shell sounded. The eighteen other merkids were already seated at their desks—even Rocky Ridge, who was almost always late. Their teacher, Mrs. Karp, raised one green eyebrow at Echo and Shelly but didn't count them as being tardy. Echo let out a sigh of relief as the first lesson began.

"Who knows what it is called when a creature changes so that it looks completely different?" Mrs. Karp asked. "Here's a hint: It's sometimes called the stages of life."

A pretty blond mergirl named Pearl Swamp raised her hand. "Do these stages have anything to do with the Plaza Hotel's famous theater?" The Plaza was a fancy hotel in Trident City that often had well-known actors and actresses perform plays on its jewel-studded stage.

Mrs. Karp stared at Pearl for a mer-minute before shaking her head.

Echo's friend Kiki Coral, the smallest mergirl in class, raised her hand. "Are you talking about metamorphosis?"

Mrs. Karp slapped her marble desk with her white tail. "Exactly!" she said.

Echo smiled at Kiki. Even though Kiki was tiny, she was probably the smartest merstudent in the whole class.

"Another way to describe metamorphosis is 'life cycles,'" Mrs. Karp continued. "Crabs have very interesting life cycles. Later this week, we'll write reports on our favorite crabs." The class groaned, but Mrs. Karp continued. "For now, let's move slowly to the back of the classroom so I can explain the crab's developmental stages."

Despite Mrs. Karp's instructions, Rocky zoomed through the room and created a wave that washed Echo's seaweed homework right off her desk. Echo shook her head. She usually thought Rocky was cute, but today he was a pain. After picking up her homework, she followed the rest of the class to the display of crab eggs.

"These eggs are in the first stage of the crab's life cycle," Mrs. Karp told them. "Eventually they will reach the second stage by developing into larvae called zoea. You will see that stage tomor- row when we start our reports, but for now here is a picture."

Mrs. Karp kept talking about the other phases of a crab's life, but Echo's mind wandered to the amazing thing she'd found under the rock. Did it really belong to a human? How long had it been there? And most importantly, what was it?

Maybe it was for capturing how something looked. Echo had heard such things were called photographs. She'd also read in *MerStyle* magazine that humans could talk to one another from half an ocean away. What if the object was something that would allow her to talk to humans? Or maybe it was a music-making machine! Shelly's grandpa, who ran Trident City's People Museum, had told her that such things existed. Maybe Kiki would come over to see it. After all, Kiki was really smart. She might know if it was used by humans. Echo hoped people used it for something totally wavy! Maybe—

"Echo Reef!" Mrs. Karp said sharply. "Can you tell us the name of the crab's final stage of life?"

"Um, I . . ." Echo didn't know what to say.

"Please pay attention!" Mrs. Karp said sternly.

Before Echo could say anything else, Pearl squealed, "Mrs. Karp! Look at what Rocky did!"

3

Feeling Crabby

I DON'T SEE WHY MRS. KARP IS making me help you hunt for crab eggs," Echo complained to Rocky after school. "I have Tail Flippers practice, and there is something really important I need to do at home."

She hoped they would find the eggs

quickly so she wouldn't miss a mer-minute of Tail Flippers practice. Coach Barnacle was very strict about showing up on time.

"It's not my fault you were daydreaming in class today," Rocky said. "And I have stuff to do too. I'm supposed to be at Shell Wars practice."

"But you're the one who ate Mrs. Karp's crab eggs!" Echo snapped as a sea lamprey slithered past her.

Rocky shrugged. "What can I say? I was hungry," he said.

Echo sighed. It was no use arguing with Rocky, so she looked around MerPark for any floating eggs. Some crabs released their eggs right into the water, so finding them wouldn't be easy. They could be any-where in the whole wide ocean!

"There are some zoea," Rocky said, pointing to small, wormlike creatures near the ocean floor.

"But we're looking for eggs," Echo reminded him crossly. "Honestly, you need to focus so we can finish."

"Sweet seaweed, you really *weren't* pay-ing attention," Rocky told her. "Crab eggs hatch into larvae called zoea. If there are larvae, maybe the eggs are close by."

Echo was so embarrassed. She really hadn't heard Mrs. Karp say any of that. She promised herself that she would listen better tomorrow, but right now they had to find some crab eggs. The sooner they found the eggs, the faster she could head to Tail Flippers practice, and the quicker she could swim home. She couldn't wait to admire her new find!

"Look!" Echo cried. Floating near a statue of a make-believe merperson named Mapella was a cluster of eggs.

Rocky flipped his brown tail into high gear and caught the eggs inside a glass jar. "Mission egg search is complete!"

"Thank Neptune!" Echo said as she turned to leave. She didn't even wave or say good-bye to Rocky. She just swam as quickly as she could to Tail Flippers practice.

Practice was even harder than she had expected. Coach Barnacle had all the mer-girls do lots of stretches and three times as

many tail flips as usual. He even asked Echo to try a very tricky kind of spin called a Scale Dropper. By the time she swam back to her shell that evening, Echo was totally pooped! But she was still excited to look at her treasure.

Crystal was floating by the front door, tapping her pink tail on the sandy floor. "I need to talk to you!" she snapped.

But Echo didn't stop to chat. She knew that her sister probably just wanted to boss her around since their parents were still at work.

"Later," Echo said as she soared down the hall to her room. She had been waiting all day to admire her new find. Finally she was going to get the chance!

Inside her room, Echo moved the sponge chair and peered behind it. But instead of seeing the amazing object she'd hidden earlier, she saw . . . nothing. Nothing but a big, empty space!

"AAHH!" Echo screamed. "It's gone!"

4

Mine!

THAT'S WHAT I NEED TO talk to you about," Crystal said from the doorway.

"Were we robbed?" Echo asked in disbelief. Nothing else was out of place in her small room, but her special object was missing! Robbery was extremely rare among merfolk, but it was still possible.

"No, we weren't robbed. *You* stole my treasure!" Crystal snapped. She pulled out the two long golden chains. As before, they floated free of each other, but were attached by a round disk.

"*Your* treasure?" Echo gasped. "How could it be *yours* when *I* found it?"

How in the ocean had her sister gotten her fins on it? Maybe Shelly had told her about it at school, though that was unlikely. Younger and older students rarely saw one another at Trident Academy.

Crystal shook her head. "I found it first. I hid it under a rock to keep it safe. I knew you must have gotten it when it was missing. So I looked around your room until I found it."

Echo couldn't believe it. She finally had something of her very own, and Crystal had taken it. She'd even searched through Echo's things to find it! Echo lunged toward her sister. "Give it back to me. It's mine!"

"No, it's not. It's mine!" Crystal said, dashing away and racing into the kitchen.

Echo had only one thing on her mind: to get her prize back! She zoomed after her sister. Echo was going so fast she couldn't slow down, even when she got to the kitchen table. She slid across the top of the table, still reaching for her sister. Unfortunately, Crystal had already made dinner: a big shell bowl of clam casserole, cups of seaweed juice, and sea-lettuce salad. Echo's crash sent all the food floating, along with the tableware.

Half the clam casserole landed in Crystal's face, so she didn't see Echo grabbing the prize. But Crystal must have felt the tug as Echo pried it from her fingers. "Leave it alone!" Crystal snapped.

"It's mine!" Echo growled, but she lost her grip on the treasure when Crystal splashed the seaweed juice. Seaweed juice didn't sting, but it could turn your face an awful green color.

Echo scrambled after the treasure once more, this time bumping into Crystal. The two mergirls rolled on the floor, crashing into the family's food storage trunk. The trunk's lid popped open, and white sea-whip pudding, ribbon worms, pickled sea cucumbers, and crab popovers floated across the kitchen. Crystal grabbed a handful of leftover ribbon worms and threw them at Echo. Echo tossed back two crab popovers. She was reaching for more food to throw at her sister when she heard a shout.

"What is going on here?"

Echo and Crystal turned to see that their mother, Dr. Eleanor Reef, was home from her job as director of the Conservatory for the Preservation of Sea Horses and Swordfish. She floated in the doorway with a shocked look on her face.

"Oops," Echo said.

She looked around their usually tidy kitchen and couldn't believe the mess. Their dinner was a blob on the floor, broken shells and leftovers floated near the ceiling, and her sister's hair even had a crab popover sticking out of it. Echo was ashamed that she'd been scuffling with her sister . . . and even more embarrassed by the mess. How had it happened so quickly?

"She tried to steal the special object I found," Crystal explained. "I discovered it last week and hid it behind our shell."

"But I found it under a rock this morning," Echo said. "It's mine!"

Dr. Reef held out her hand. "Until you merladies can learn to get along, whatever it is that you're fighting about belongs to me."

"But—"

"No buts," their mother said. "Give me that thing and get this mess cleaned up. Right now!"

5

Warts

I

T'S ALL CRYSTAL'S FAULT," ECHO
told Kiki and Shelly the next day
in the science lab. They were supposed to be sketching the different stages
of the crab's life cycle, but so far Echo had
only drawn the first three: eggs, zoea, and
megalopae. Luckily, Mrs. Karp was too

busy helping a merstudent named Morgan on the other side of the lab to notice.

Shelly scrunched her nose as she drew a leg on a juvenile crab. "Well, if Crystal did find it first," she whispered, "then it sort of belongs to her."

Echo put her right hand on her hip. "Crystal might not have even been telling the truth."

"Does Crystal usually lie?" Kiki asked.

Echo frowned. "No, but that doesn't mean she didn't this time."

"What exactly does this object look like, anyway?" Kiki asked.

"It has two chains connected by this pretty golden disk," Echo explained.

"Is the disk big?" Kiki asked.

Echo shook her head and made a small loop with her thumb and forefinger to show the right size. "Do you know if it might have belonged to a human?" she asked hopefully.

But Kiki didn't get a chance to answer, because Mrs. Karp suddenly appeared beside them. "Let's get to work," she told the mergirls.

Echo tried to draw the next two stages, juvenile and adult, but she was still so mad at Crystal that she couldn't concentrate.

Then she heard Pearl screech, "Get that thing away from me!"

Rocky held a spotted reef crab in front of Pearl's face. "I thought you'd like it," he said with a grin. "It's kind of pretty."

Echo knew Rocky was just being silly; he didn't really think Pearl liked crabs. Everyone knew she hated anything slimy or dirty.

Pearl took another look at the light-brown crab with its large red spots and knocked the creature away. "Ew! I don't like things with claws," she said.

The crab soared through the water—right onto Echo's head. "Ahhh!" she squealed. "Get it off me!"

Mrs. Karp quickly lifted the crab off Echo's head and frowned at Pearl. Pearl turned her pointy nose up in the water and sniffed before dipping her orange sea pen in octopus ink to continue sketching.

"Yuck! Hey, Mrs. Karp, do crabs give

you warts if they touch your head?" Rocky asked.

Echo gasped, but Mrs. Karp reassured her. "No, you do not get warts from crabs or any other sea creature."

Echo was relieved. She wasn't exactly sure what warts were, but they didn't sound good.

"Mrs. Karp, look!" Kiki said. "I think the crab eggs that Rocky and Echo found are hatching."

Mrs. Karp smiled. "Oh, how wonderful. Let's all watch."

The entire merclass gathered at the back of the classroom around the glass jar.

Mrs. Karp squinted through her glasses. "Up close these crab eggs look different from others I've seen," she said. "Where did you find them, Rocky and Echo?"

"In MerPark," Rocky told her. "There were some zoea floating nearby."

Mrs. Karp didn't say anything, but when the first egg cracked open, she held her arms out and gently pushed the students away from the jar. "Class, please back up. These are *not* crab eggs."

"What are they?" Shelly asked.

"They are Sloane's viperfish," Mrs. Karp said. The class gasped. Every merkid knew to stay away from viperfish and their barbed teeth.

Pearl took one look at the tiny newly hatched viperfish and screamed. "Oh my Neptune! Rocky and Echo are trying to kill us! Save me!"

6

Accidentally

YOU SHOULD HAVE SEEN IT! This whole school of viperfish almost ripped my head off!" Pearl waved her hands in the water as she told a group of fourth graders in the cafeteria all about her near-death experience.

"No wavy way!" Echo muttered as she

sat at her usual corner table. "Did Pearl really think that a baby viperfish was going to eat her up?"

Shelly put her tray down and slid her blue tail under the polished granite table with the gold Trident Academy logo in the center. "I'm pretty sure they don't eat merpeople."

Kiki took a seat beside her merfriends. "But they are kind of creepy-looking. Echo, how did you mistake viperfish eggs for crab eggs?"

Echo shrugged. "I was in a hurry to get to Tail Flippers practice, and Rocky was late for Shell Wars practice," she said. "Anybody could have done it. It was an innocent mistake."

Shelly swallowed a big bite of her boxfish burger before nodding. "Just like accidentally taking your sister's treasure was a mistake."

"It's not her treasure! It's mine!" Echo snapped. Shelly was starting to make Echo mad. "Besides, Crystal is always bossing me around. She thinks she's so much better than me, just because she's older. And I never have anything that's my very own. If you had a sister, you'd understand."

Shelly didn't say anything. She just took another bite of her burger. Echo felt a tiny bit bad. She knew that Shelly had always wanted a brother or a sister, and Echo hoped she hadn't hurt her friend's feelings.

"But I don't have any sisters either," Kiki told Echo. "And while what you say might be true, I am pretty sure that if you want to get that treasure back, you're going to have to tell your sister you're sorry."

"But I don't have anything to be sorry for!" Echo said loudly.

"Maybe not," Kiki said, "but your mom is never going to give you back your treasure if you guys aren't getting along."

Echo thought about that while she munched on yellow splash lichen chips. Maybe Kiki had a point.

And perhaps Echo didn't really have to *be* sorry. Maybe she just had to *pretend* she was sorry. She was willing to do almost anything to get that treasure back!

But she didn't tell her friends that. They probably wouldn't understand how she felt about Crystal, since they didn't have sisters of their own. Instead Echo said, "You may be right, but Crystal is really mad. What can I do to show my mom that Crystal and I are friends again?"

Shelly put her burger down. "What if you made a special treat for Crystal? Sometimes when I'm grumpy my grandfather will make me some cup coral candy to cheer me up."

"If that doesn't work, maybe you could clean her room or buy her a gift," Kiki said. "My brothers get mad at each other a lot, and sometimes that's how they make up."

Echo nodded. She knew Kiki had seventeen brothers. At least some of them were probably mad at one another at any given time.

Echo stuffed a whole handful of chips into her mouth and crunched. The more she thought about it, the simpler it seemed. As long as she showed her mother that she was doing her best to get along with Crystal, Mrs. Reef would be so impressed with her  behavior that she would give the object back to Echo. Crystal wouldn't be able to touch it!

"Those are great ideas," Echo said. "Do you want to help me after school?" She smiled as her friends nodded their heads.

Echo could hardly wait to get home! It was a great plan. What could possibly go wrong?

7

Crystal's Mess

YOU GUYS ARE TRUE FRIENDS
for helping me today," Echo
told Kiki and Shelly. "I'm just
lucky that Coach Barnacle canceled Tail
Flippers practice. Plus, Crystal won't be
home until later, so we have time to put
our plan into action."

Kiki and Shelly grinned as they floated into Echo's shell. "We're here to help," Kiki said. "Do you want to make her a treat? I just learned how to make cup coral candy."

Echo shook her head. "No, my mom said I'm not allowed in the kitchen today. Crystal and I made a mess in there yesterday."

Shelly plopped onto a big barrel sponge couch in Echo's living room. "What else do you want to do for Crystal? What if you make her a nice seaweed 'I'm sorry' card?"

"I liked Kiki's idea about cleaning Crystal's room," Echo said. "Her room is always really messy. Come on, I'll show you."

"Maybe this isn't such a good idea," Shelly whispered as the girls floated down the hallway.

Shelly, Echo, and Kiki squeezed into Crystal's room and looked around. Dirty shells and crumpled seaweed littered the floor. Clothes were piled in every corner and on the end of her bed. Crystal was one of Trident Academy's best artists, so half-finished art projects lined one wall and big chunks of clay were thrown about the floor, ready to be made into sculptures.

"Shelly might be right," Kiki said. "Should we really be touching Crystal's stuff?"

"But she hates to clean her room," Echo said. "My mom is always nagging her about it. Crystal will be so happy if we do it for her." What Echo really meant was

that their mom would be happy with Echo. And that meant she could get her treasure back. At least, she hoped so.

Kiki shook her head. "Crystal is even messier than Wanda." Kiki had been Wanda's roommate in the dorm at the beginning of the school year.

"Let's bubble down and do this, then," Shelly said, scrunching her nose at the stinky shells.

In two tail shakes, the mergirls had Crystal's clothes folded and a stack of shells to take to the kitchen. Art projects were placed neatly on a shelf, and all the crumpled seaweed schoolwork was straightened into a nice, tidy mound.

"What should we do with these lumps

of clay?" Kiki asked, pointing to the heaps scattered across the room.

"Let's pile them up in that corner," Echo suggested.

"Are you sure?" Shelly asked. "Do you think she's making something with them? Maybe we shouldn't touch them."

Echo waved the idea away. "I'm sure it's fine. They're only bits of clay, after all." Echo just wanted to finish so she could have her treasure back. She stacked the clay into neat piles in a corner, one on top of the other. The big pieces stuck together easily, so Crystal's room looked much nicer.

It took them a few merminutes, but finally the three friends stopped working and smiled at one another.

★ **49** ★

"This is the cleanest room in the entire merkingdom!" Shelly announced.

"Crystal is going to be so happy," Kiki agreed.

Just then Crystal floated into the room.

"Surprise!" Echo yelled. She crossed her fingers and her tail fins behind her back. "I'm sorry for taking your treasure, so I decided to clean your room for you! And Kiki and Shelly helped."

But Crystal looked horrified. "ECHO!" she screeched, rushing over to the lumps of clay in the corner. "You ruined my project for Parent Night!"

8

Destroyed

I CAN'T BELIEVE YOU DESTROYED my sculpture," Crystal said between sobs.

"I'm so sorry," Echo said. "I didn't mean to do it. I was only trying to make you happy by cleaning your room." *And make Mom happy by being nice to you,* she thought.

"It's true," Shelly said, putting a hand on Echo's shoulder.

"Actually, it was my fault we ruined your project," Kiki said.

"Mine too. Kiki and I told Echo to pile the clay in the corner like that," Shelly chimed in. "We didn't know it was for Parent Night."

Echo looked at her friends. She couldn't believe they were trying to take the blame for her. There was no wavy way she'd let them!

"No, it was my fault," Echo said, shaking her head. "I suggested that we stack them up. I thought they were just lumps of clay."

"What am I going to do? I'll flunk art class for sure!" Crystal moaned.

Echo felt horrible. Despite the fact that

she really did want the treasure all for herself, she hadn't meant for this to happen.

Then she realized something that made her feel even worse. Her parents would never give her back the object if they found out that she had ruined Crystal's art project. Echo had to do something—and fast!

She shook her head. "You won't flunk class. Since the whole thing was my fault, I'll help you fix it."

"But Parent Night is tomorrow!" Crystal said with a sob. "And Mom and Dad put me in charge of supper tonight. There's no way I'll finish everything in time!"

"Shelly and I can make supper for you," Kiki offered. Echo gave her friends a grateful smile.

"And we can work all evening and after school tomorrow," Echo said. "Don't worry, we'll do it together." Echo might not always get along with Crystal, but she hated to see her sister cry.

Crystal wiped her tears. "Do you really think so?"

Echo held her arms out to her sister. "I'm not as talented an artist as you, but Miss Haniver says I do have potential."

Crystal shrugged. "Okay, I guess we can give it a try."

In just a few minutes, Shelly and Kiki were hard at work on dinner in the kitchen while Echo and her sister sat on the floor of Crystal's room.

"This is what you should do," Crystal

explained. She showed Echo how to use her hands to smooth the outside of a big lump of clay. When Echo tried it, hers didn't look half as good as Crystal's.

Crystal glanced up from the clay she was shaping. "Hmmm," she told Echo. "Try holding your hands like this."

After they had been shaping and smoothing for a while, Crystal took several of the smooth lumps and put them together. Echo's eyes grew wide.

"No wavy way!" Echo squealed. "Are you making a megamouth shark?"

Crystal smiled and rubbed a muddy hand on her nose. "Yep!"

"It's totally wavy," Echo said truthfully. "You're really good at this, Crystal."

"Thanks." Crystal smiled. "You're becoming a pretty great artist yourself!"

After only an hour, Echo and Crystal were covered in clay. Even their tails changed from bright pink to a muddy, dull coral color. By suppertime, Echo's arms ached and she was hungry for the delicious meal that Kiki and Shelly had left on the table.

"What in the ocean have you two been up to?" Echo's father asked when he saw his merdaughters covered in clay.

Echo froze. She didn't want to explain what had happened to Crystal's art project. Her mom and dad would be mad if they found out what she'd done.

She waited for Crystal to tell them the whole story, but her sister just said, "Echo is helping me with a sculpture. It's for Parent Night."

Echo's mother smiled. "I'm so happy you two are getting along. If this continues, then perhaps we can discuss the return of your find."

Though she was dogfish tired from working so hard, the mention of the treasure made Echo's heart race.

"This is the best dinner I've ever tasted," Mrs. Reef exclaimed.

Echo started to explain that Kiki and Shelly had made it, but Mr. Reef chimed in. "Since you girls have been working so hard, I will take your turn at cleanup tonight." Crystal and Echo exchanged smiles.

When they were finished eating, Crystal said, "Come on, Echo. Let's get back to work."

"Thank you for not telling Dad that I messed up your project," Echo told Crystal when they were in Crystal's room.

Crystal shrugged. "Sisters have to stick together. And I never did thank you for cleaning my room. It looks great!"

"Shelly and Kiki helped too," Echo explained. "I'm just sorry that I ruined your sculpture."

Crystal nodded. "I had everything in a rough form. There was no way for you to know."

"I'm glad I can help fix it," Echo said.

Crystal smiled and the two girls got back to work, with Crystal shaping and Echo smoothing. To Echo's surprise, it was a lot of fun. Crystal told stories about the silly merboys in her art class, and Echo told Crystal how Rocky had eaten the crab eggs. The sisters giggled until their fins ached. It was just like when they had played together as small fry.

Finally the shark's head was completed. "We still have a lot of work left to do," Crystal announced. "Tomorrow afternoon we'll work on the body. I just hope we can finish in time."

"Don't worry," Echo said. "I won't let you down."

Star

PEARL WAS GIGGLING IN THE cafeteria the next day. "I'm going to be the star of Parent Night," she bragged to the mergirls at her lunch table. "I've been practicing my Tail Flippers routine like crazy. Watch this."

Pearl did the unthinkable. She did a

Scale Dropper right in the middle of the cafeteria. Only she didn't quite get the difficult flip-and-spin combination just right. She did more spinning than flipping and managed to smack into a cart filled with bottles of kelp juice. Juice and shells soared everywhere. A large bucket of juice even landed on Mr. Fangtooth's bald head. The cafeteria worker had never looked more angry . . . and he was known for being grumpy.

Rocky and his table full of merboys roared with laughter. "Pearl is a flipping disaster!" Rocky teased.

"Oh no!" Shelly gasped. "Should we help Pearl?"

But the mergirls didn't get the chance. Mr. Fangtooth removed the bucket and handed Pearl a magnificent feather duster worm. "Clean this mess up," he growled.

Pearl frowned at the fluffy worm before taking it between two fingers. "Ick! My mother wouldn't like me touching this creature."

Mr. Fangtooth glared at Pearl. "Would you like me to ask your mother?"

Pearl quickly shook her head. "No, I'll wipe it up." She held the feather duster as far from her body as possible and cleaned up the kelp juice with the worm's fluffy tentacles.

Kiki took a bite of her yellow splash lichen chips and shook her head. "I think Pearl has some more practicing to do before Parent Night tonight."

"Oh no!" Echo gasped. "I totally forgot! If I don't go to Tail Flippers practice today, I won't be able to perform at Parent Night."

"I thought you were helping Crystal finish her art project after school," Kiki said after taking a sip of kelp juice.

"Well, I'm supposed to," Echo said sadly. "If I don't help her, there's no way she'll finish in time. But that means I won't be able to perform tonight. I just hope Coach Barnacle won't kick me off the team!"

Shelly and Kiki looked at each other. "But you practiced so much," Shelly said. "There must be something you can do."

Echo shook her head. She took a bite of her hagfish jelly sandwich, but it was hard to swallow. "I promised Crystal I would help her. And a promise is a promise."

"Plus, if you help Crystal, you still might get your human object back," Kiki suggested.

Echo brightened a little. "You're right," she agreed, taking a sip of kelp juice. She knew Kiki was trying to cheer her up, but Echo's heart was broken. She had really wanted her parents to see her perform.

"Shelly and I should go to the People Museum after school," Kiki said, changing the subject.

"Why?" Shelly asked.

"To see if we can figure out what Echo and Crystal found. Maybe it's not even human," Kiki said. "Shelly, you saw it, right?"

Shelly nodded. "Yes."

Echo sipped her kelp drink. Whatever it was, if she had to miss performing with the Tail Flippers, she really hoped she could have that object back.

10

A Promise

BE CAREFUL! DON'T DROP IT!" Crystal cried later that evening. Echo and her sister carried an enormous megamouth shark sculpture into the big entrance hall to Trident Academy.

"I'm being careful," Echo said.

"Sorry," Crystal said. "I shouldn't have snapped. I'm just really tired."

Echo nodded. She was worn out too. Carrying the heavy sculpture made her arms feel like floppy jellyfish tentacles, but she was determined to get it safely to wherever it had to go.

Miss Haniver, their art teacher, had transformed the school's front hall into an art gallery. There were displays of artwork from students of all different grades. Echo saw her own class's mollusk sculptures. They were nowhere near as fancy as the shark and whale ones Crystal's fifth-grade class had made, which Echo had to admit were pretty spectacular.

Crystal and Echo carefully set the

sculpture down on a large marble table in the center of the room. Looking around at the other pieces of art, Echo realized that Crystal's was by far the best. Echo felt proud of her sister and how hard they had worked together.

"Perfect," Crystal said. She slowly floated around the sculpture, examining it from all angles. "It just needs one more thing."

She held up a small piece of seaweed. Written on the seaweed were the words ART BY CRYSTAL AND ECHO REEF.

Echo's heart flopped around like a fish in her chest. "But Crystal, I don't deserve that. I almost ruined the whole thing! Plus, I only helped smooth the clay. You did all the real work."

Crystal shook her head and smiled. "It doesn't matter. I wouldn't have finished without you. This is as much yours as it is mine. Sisters share!"

Just then an announcement came over the conch shell from Headmaster Hermit. "Welcome to Trident Academy's 975th Parent Night," he boomed. "Please proceed to the auditorium for our opening remarks and entertainment."

Crystal glanced at the doorway. A steady stream of merparents and merstudents floated in. "I hope Mom and Dad get here in time to see you perform," she said. "Speaking of which, don't you need to get ready?"

Echo hadn't told her sister that she wouldn't be performing with the Tail Flippers. Before she could say anything, one of Crystal's friends came up and hugged her. "Your sculpture is the best!"

"Thanks, Fay. Your clay narwhal is adorable," Crystal told her classmate.

Echo spotted Kiki from across the room and waved. "See you later, Crystal," she said. "I'm going to say hello to Kiki." Echo knew Kiki might be feeling lonely because her parents weren't going to be able to come for Parent Night. They lived too far away to make the trip. Plus, Echo didn't feel like telling Crystal why she was missing her Tail Flippers performance.

"Hi," Kiki said. "I just saw Crystal's sculpture. It looks fabulous!"

Echo grinned. "I know. It was hard work, but we did it. Plus, she even put my name on it!"

"That's wavy," Kiki said. "So she's not mad at you anymore?"

"She doesn't seem to be," Echo said. She hated to admit it, but she'd actually had a good time working with Crystal. It was like when they'd played together as small fry.

"I have something awesome to tell you," Kiki began, but she was interrupted by the pounding of sharkskin drums.

"It will have to wait until after the program," Echo said. "It's starting now." The mergirls scooted into the auditorium just as the lights dimmed. Echo tried to see if her parents or Shelly had arrived, but it was too dark. Echo and Kiki took seats near the doorway.

The program lasted quite a while. First the Trident Academy Pep Band played a seashell rhapsody that had everyone tapping their fins. The Shell Wars team did a small scrimmage. Echo cheered when Shelly scored a goal.

"I love that song," Kiki sighed after the chorus performed "Ode to Seaweed."

"Me too," Echo said. "This is so much fun." But her heart sank when the Tail Flippers bounced onto the stage without her. As they flipped in time to the music, Echo couldn't help wishing she was up there too.

After the program, everyone poured out into the school's enormous entrance hall for refreshments and to look at the art show. Coach Barnacle floated up to Echo with a huge frown on his face.

"Echo Reef!" he boomed, staring down at her. "You'd better have a very good excuse for why you didn't perform with the Tail Flippers tonight!"

11

Friends

ECHO WAS STILL TRYING TO figure out what to say to Coach Barnacle when her parents and Crystal swam over to them. "Echo! We were worried when we didn't see you with the other Tail Flippers," her father exclaimed. "What happened?"

Crystal nodded. "I was looking forward to seeing that special new flip of yours."

Echo didn't know what to say. Kiki saved her by explaining, "Echo couldn't perform because she didn't go to practice today. It was the rules."

"But why did you miss practice?" her father asked.

"Yes, Echo," Coach Barnacle said, thumping the ocean floor with his brown tail. "Why did you miss practice? You know I can kick you off the team for missing both practice and the performance tonight."

Echo gasped. Her worst fear was to get kicked off the Tail Flippers team!

"She missed it because she was helping me finish my sculpture," Crystal told the adults.

"Oh, Echo," their mother said. "You gave up performing just to help your sister?"

Coach Barnacle brushed a tear from his eye. "That's so sweet." Then he cleared his throat and threw his hands up in the air. "Just make sure it doesn't happen again!"

"Yes, sir," Echo said quickly. "Thanks for giving me another chance, Coach." She let out a sigh of relief as Coach Barnacle floated away to speak to Mayor Ridge.

Mrs. Reef gave her younger daughter a big hug. "Echo, I'm so proud of you. You've really shown me that you can get along with your sister. In fact," she continued, "I think you're both behaving well enough to have this back." Her mother pulled the human treasure out of her merpouch and offered it to them.

Echo shook her head and backed away. She took a deep breath and thought about what Crystal had said to her. *Sisters share.*

"No, give it to Crystal. She found it first." Echo bit her lip. It was a very hard thing for her to say. She loved human objects so much, but she knew it was the right thing to do.

Crystal frowned. "But you gave up performing with the Tail Flippers just to help me. You deserve it."

"Don't worry," Kiki interrupted. "Shelly and I know how to solve this problem."

"You do?" Echo asked.

"We do," Shelly said, swimming up

beside them. She was still dressed in her Shell Wars uniform. "Grandfather rattled around in all his storage closets and found a human object that looked just like yours. Kiki had seen one in a book before."

"That's what I wanted to tell you earlier," Kiki told Echo.

"Do you know what it is?" Echo's mother asked.

Kiki grinned. "Yes, I think so. May I see it?" Echo's mother nodded and handed the treasure to Kiki.

Kiki grabbed the round disk in the center and pulled. It popped into two pieces. "Oh no!" Crystal cried. "You broke it!"

Kiki shook her head. "No, it was made for sharing. Look closer. See what it says?"

Shelly, Echo, Crystal, and Mr. and Mrs. Reef gathered around the treasure. Each piece of the broken circle had a jagged edge where it fit into the other piece. Both parts had a chain attached. One said BEST. And the other said FRIENDS. Echo couldn't believe she hadn't noticed the tiny words before!

"It's a friendship necklace," explained Kiki. "One person wears one part of it. The other person wears the other half. Humans use them to show that they're friends for life!"

Echo looked at Crystal. She was sorry

that she'd fought with her sister over a human object—especially one that was made for sharing.

Their mother laughed and put one chain over Echo's head and the other over Crystal's. "Well, that's perfect. I'm glad my daughters are friends again."

Echo grinned and gave Crystal a hug. "*Best* friends!"

Class Reports

ORANGE FIDDLER CRAB

By Shelly Siren

The thing I like best about the orange

fiddler crab is that one of its claws is huge compared to its body. It lives

near water in mud or sand and is awake during the day. It digs a hole to live in, complete with escape routes.

JAPANESE SPIDER CRAB
By Echo Reef

The Japanese spider crab is the biggest of all crabs. Its legs are twice as long as most mermen are tall. It also lives to be about one hundred years old. I think it would be great fun to ride on the back of a Japanese spider crab!

GHOST CRAB
By Rocky Ridge

The ghost crab is the coolest crab. It hides during the day and comes out just before dark to hunt. It will eat anything, even other crabs! I wonder if it can disappear like a real ghost.

PORCELAIN CRAB
By Pearl Swamp

Crabs are very ugly. But the porcelain crab is a pretty bluish color, even though the rest of it is kind of creepy-looking. Can you believe the porcelain crab will shed a claw if it needs to escape? Then it will grow the claw back. Isn't that just icky?

COMMON LOBSTER

By Kiki Coral

This lobster doesn't begin to have babies until it is six years old. The problem is that

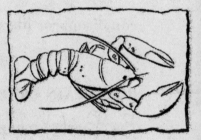

people like to eat this kind of lobster, and because it takes so long to start having babies, it is in danger of disappearing from the ocean.

The Mermaid Tales Song

REFRAIN:

Let the water roar

Deep down we're swimming along

Twirling, swirling, singing the mermaid song.

VERSE 1:

Shelly flips her tail

Racing, diving, chasing a whale

Twirling, swirling, singing the mermaid song.

VERSE 2:

Pearl likes to shine

Oh my Neptune, she looks so fine

Twirling, swirling, singing the mermaid song.

VERSE 3:

Shining Echo flips her tail

Backward and forward without fail

Twirling, swirling, singing the mermaid song.

VERSE 4:

Amazing Kiki

Far from home and floating so free

Twirling, swirling, singing the mermaid song.

Author's Note

I HAVE TWO BROTHERS, BUT I ALWAYS wanted to have a sister, like Echo. My brothers and I did have plenty of arguments growing up, but we managed to have good times too. We had to dry the dishes every night after supper, and we would sing songs to make it more fun. In the summer, we would go for long bike rides and take picnic lunches with us. We would also spend many afternoons playing baseball with all the kids in our neighborhood. In the wintertime, we made snowmen. Once, when it snowed a lot, we made forts and tunnels that we crawled through with our dog, Spike. It would have been nice to have a sister, but my brothers were pretty fun! You can find out more about me at www.debbiedadey.com, and I hope your parents will like me at www.Facebook.com/debbiedadey.

Your mermaid friend,
Debbie Dadey

Glossary

BARNACLE: Adult barnacles affix themselves to one spot, like a rock or ship.

BARREL SPONGE: This sponge can get quite large, but its surface is hard.

BOXFISH: The spotted boxfish will ooze poison slime from its skin to keep predators from eating it. Luckily, mermaids are immune to the poison.

CLAM: There are 14,000 types of clams. They have a shell that connects on one side.

CONCH: If you go to the beach and someone

offers to sell you a conch shell, please don't buy it. Conch are at risk for extinction because people have collected their beautiful shells for many years.

CORAL: Daisy coral grows to look like a field of beautiful flowers.

CRAB: Marine crabs are arthropods and tend to live alone on the bottom of the ocean.

CUP CORAL: The Devonshire cup coral is one of the few corals that live alone. It will attach itself to a rock or even a shipwreck.

HAGFISH: This fish should be named "slime-fish" because it can squirt slime out of the pores on the side of its body!

JELLYFISH: The deep-sea jellyfish looks like it is wearing a ballet tutu!

LICHEN: Black tufted lichen is found on

sunny rocks and has small bumps on its branch tips.

MAGNIFICENT FEATHER DUSTER: This worm has lots of brown-and-white tentacles that look like an old-fashioned feather duster.

MEGAMOUTH SHARK: This huge shark is thought to attract food with a glowing mouth.

MOLLUSK: Oysters and octopuses are part of this family of creatures.

NARWHAL: This thirteen-to-twenty-foot-long whale lives in polar waters and is known mostly for its unicorn-like tusk.

OCTOPUS: When an octopus is threatened, it will squirt an ink-like substance.

ORANGE SEA PEN: This creature looks like

an old-fashioned pen made from a sharpened feather.

PLANKTON: Tiny creatures that float with the ocean currents and live near the surface are called plankton. Some plankton glow!

RIBBON WORM: This thin worm can grow to be as long as the width of a football field!

SAILFISH: The sailfish's long, spearlike jaw looks similar to the swordfish's upper jaw, but the sailfish also has a huge, sail-like dorsal fin. It folds the fin away for fast swimming.

SEA CUCUMBERS: The deep-sea cucumber crawls along the ocean floor, eating the organic matter it finds.

SEA LAMPREY: This eel-like creature has no jaws. It uses a sucker that attaches to other fish to suck out food. Due to poisoning and trapping, it is becoming rare.

SEA LETTUCE: Sea lettuce grows along the shoreline in most parts of the world. It is eaten by animals and people.

SEAWEED: Can you grow twenty-four inches in one day? Giant kelp, a type of seaweed, can!

SHELL: Many animals, including oysters, use shells as a home. You may find pretty shells washed up on the shore.

SPONGE: Sponges are common on rocky reefs, shipwrecks, and coral reefs. They can be circular or tubelike.

SPOTTED REEF CRAB: This slow-moving crab likes to feed at night, which means it is nocturnal.

VIPERFISH: Sloane's viperfish is a long, thin

FIND OUT WHAT HAPPENS IN THE NEXT . . .

Mermaid Tales

★Debbie Dadey★

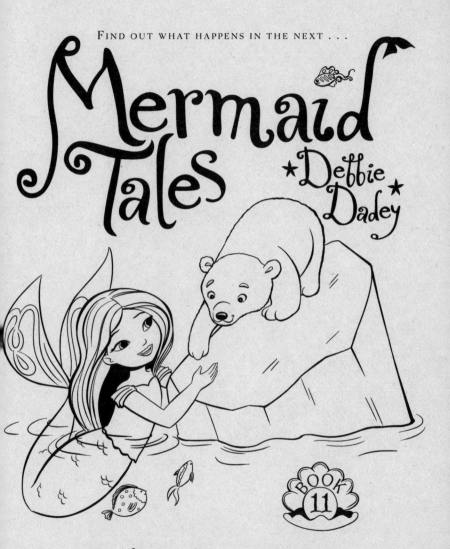

BOOK 11

The Polar Bear Express

Splat!

"Five arms stretch out wide
No brains; no blood; velvety
Starfish cling to life."

"I really like that," Kiki Coral told her teacher.

"It's a haiku," Mrs. Karp explained.

"Five claps for the first line, then seven, then five for the last line."

"Boring," Pearl Swamp whispered under her breath. Mrs. Karp peered through her tiny glasses at Pearl, who slid down in her seat.

"Do you think the Rays' music is boring?" Mrs. Karp asked Pearl.

Pearl sat up straight and tossed her long blond hair behind her shoulder. "Of course not!" The Rays were the most famous boy band in the entire ocean. They had sung at Pearl's last birthday party.

"Did you know that many of the Rays' songs are poems?" Mrs. Karp said. "Of course, they are different from a haiku."

"Really?" asked Shelly Siren. Shelly

was the only student at Trident Academy who had actually performed with the Rays at Pearl's party. When their backup singer had gotten sick, Shelly had filled in for her.

Mrs. Karp nodded and surprised her entire third-grade class by singing one of the Rays' songs.

"*Shark, the sharpnose sevengill,*
　　lived near to me.
We swam together every day
And became the best of friends.
Then someone told Shark he
　　should eat me.
And now I miss him terribly
But our friendship had to end.

Shark, the sharpnose sevengill,

lived near to me.

I'll always treasure our friendship

And hope someday he'll see

That sharks and merfolks can be

friends.

One day it will be.

But until that day, I guess I'll say

Shark, I miss you still."

Pearl rolled her eyes, but most of the class tapped their tails in time to Mrs. Karp's voice. When she finished, everyone clapped except Pearl.

"That was totally amazing!" Echo Reef said.

Mrs. Karp grinned and took a little

bow. "What do you think about poems now?" she asked Pearl.

Pearl shrugged. "I guess some poems are pretty wavy."

"I think poems should be silly," Rocky Ridge said before singing to the class in a funny voice:

"Food fights can be fun.
Especially at lunchtime.
Splat! Right in the face!"

Rocky acted out the splat and fell onto the floor.

Mrs. Karp hid her smile behind her hand, but Kiki couldn't help laughing just a little. "That was very creative,"

Mrs. Karp told Rocky, "but I hope you don't plan to have a real food fight."

Rocky shook his head, but Kiki noticed the grin on his face. Kiki knew Rocky would love to throw anything, especially food.

"You've given me a wonderful idea," Mrs. Karp told Rocky. "Everyone will write their own poem for our next class assignment. It can be a haiku or a song or whatever type you'd like. We'll talk about other kinds of poems in class tomorrow."

Pearl frowned at Rocky. "Thanks a lot!" she snapped. "More homework!"

2

Shake Your Tail

AT LUNCHTIME KIKI SLID into a round table in a corner of Trident Academy's cafeteria. Shelly and their merfriend Echo joined her.

"Wasn't it fun when Mrs. Karp sang in class?" Kiki asked.

Shelly smiled. "I didn't know she had such a nice voice."

"I love that Rays song," Echo said. "Have you heard their newest one?"

Kiki shook her head, pushed her long black hair out of her face, and took a bite of her crab casserole.

"Sing it for her, Shelly," Echo said, giving Shelly a little nudge with her shoulder.

Shelly sang,

"Shake your tail
Shake, shake, shake your tail
Let's bubble down and make like
    a whale
Shake, shake, shake your tail."

Shelly was probably the best singer in the whole school—maybe in the entire mer-kingdom. She was so good that everyone in the cafeteria stopped to listen to her. When Shelly finished, Kiki clapped and the rest of the school joined in. Everyone but Pearl.

Shelly's face turned red. She quickly scooped up a big bite of her longhorn cow-fish and ate it without looking up. Her long hair partly covered her crimson cheeks.

Pearl floated over to their table and pointed her nose up in the water. "Did you know that the Rays are performing a con-cert in Poseidon tomorrow?"

"Really?" Echo asked. Poseidon was the town right next to Trident City, where they lived.

Pearl nodded. "Yes, and my father is taking me to see them. I bet I'm the only one in the whole school who will go. The tickets are very expensive."

Shelly, Echo, and Kiki looked at one another without saying a word. Pearl's parents were rich, and they lived in one of Trident City's biggest shells. Everyone knew Pearl always got want she wanted. Many Trident City merfolk thought Pearl's parents spoiled her.

Kiki felt like telling Pearl that it wasn't nice to brag, but Pearl wasn't finished. "I'm going to write the Rays a poem song. I'll give it to them, and I bet they'll sing it just for me."

"That's great idea," Echo said.

Kiki looked at Echo in surprise. Kiki knew Echo didn't like Pearl's bragging either.

"I'm going to write a poem song too," Echo continued. "Maybe the Rays will like mine and make it famous throughout the merworld."

Pearl frowned. "But I thought of it first!"

Pearl's friend Wanda swam up beside Pearl. "It *is* a great idea. I'm going to write a song for the Rays too."

Pearl gave Wanda a dirty look and swam off to her own table, leaving a trail of bubbles behind. Wanda followed with a worried look on her face.

"Let's meet at my shell after school," Shelly told her friends. "We can work on our poems and poem songs together."

"I can bring the snacks," Kiki suggested. "I just got a trunk full of treats from home. My mom sent lots of sea cucumbers."

Unlike Shelly and Echo, who lived close to Trident Academy, Kiki's family lived far across the ocean, so she stayed in the school's dormitory. Kiki's mom often sent her care packages filled with goodies.

Shelly grinned. "Yum! I love those!"

"Oops!" Kiki said. "I forgot that I have vision practice with Madame Hippocampus after school today."

"Just come over when you're done," Shelly said.

"Hey, do you know the best part about

writing a poem song for the Rays?" Echo asked her friends.

"What?" Kiki asked.

"Making Pearl mad without even trying," Echo replied with a giggle.

All three girls turned to look at Pearl. She was staring at them from across the room with a big frown on her face.

"Oh my Neptune!" Shelly said. "We don't want to make Pearl angry at us."

Kiki nodded. "Pearl does seem to like trouble."

Echo shrugged. "I know, but how much trouble could she *really* cause us?"

Debbie Dadey

is the author and coauthor of more than one hundred and fifty children's books, including the series The Adventures of the Bailey School Kids. A former teacher and librarian, Debbie and her family split their time between Bucks County, Pennsylvania, and Sevierville, Tennessee. She hopes you'll visit www.debbiedadey.com for lots of mermaid fun.

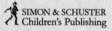

Candy Fairies

Chocolate Dreams	Rainbow Swirl	Caramel Moon
Cool Mint	Magic Hearts	Gooey Goblins
The Sugar Ball	A Valentine's Surprise	Bubble Gum Rescue
Double Dip	Jelly Bean Jumble	The Chocolate Rose
A Royal Wedding	Marshmallow Mystery	Frozen Treats
The Sugar Cup	Sweet Secrets	Taffy Trouble

Visit candyfairies.com
for games, recipes, and more!

Nancy Drew and the Clue Crew®

Test your detective skills with more Clue Crew cases!

Visit NancyDrew.com for the inside scoop!

From Aladdin · KIDS.SimonandSchuster.com

Goddess Girls

READ ABOUT ALL
YOUR FAVORITE GODDESSES!

**#17 AMPHITRITE
THE BUBBLY**

**#16 MEDUSA
THE RICH**

**#15 APHRODITE
THE FAIR**

**#14 IRIS
THE COLORFUL**

**#13 ATHENA
THE PROUD**

**#12 CASSANDRA
THE LUCKY**

**#11 PERSEPHONE
THE DARING**

**#10 PHEME
THE GOSSIP**

**#1 ATHENA
THE BRAIN**

**#6 APHRODITE
THE DIVA**

**#2 PERSEPHONE
THE PHONY**

**#7 ARTEMIS
THE LOYAL**

**#3 APHRODITE
THE BEAUTY**

**THE GIRL GAMES:
SUPER SPECIAL**

**#4 ARTEMIS
THE BRAVE**

**#8 MEDUSA
THE MEAN**

**#5 ATHENA
THE WISE**

**#9 PANDORA
THE CURIOUS**

EBOOK EDITIONS ALSO AVAILABLE

From Aladdin
KIDS.SimonandSchuster.com